“ECHOES OF THE LAUGHING FOREST”

CHAPTER CRAFTERS

Made with ♥ on the Notion Press Platform
www.notionpress.com

To Nature & Magic – For the forests that whisper, the magic that lingers, and the wild hearts that dare to listen.

To Friendship & Adventure – For those who find courage in friendship, wonder in the unknown, and light in the darkest of places.

Contents

Prologue

The Hollow was dying.

The trees, once tall and whispering with life, stood silent. Their leaves, once shimmering with magic, crumbled to dust at the slightest touch. The air, thick with the scent of damp earth and old enchantments, now carried only the weight of something broken.

At the heart of it all, the Guardian stirred. Once the protector of this sacred place, its form had become twisted, its power tainted. It had fought the curse for as long as it could, but the corruption had sunk too deep. Now, it watched as the Hollow withered around it, the magic unraveling thread by thread.

Somewhere beyond the dying trees, footsteps echoed—three sets, hesitant but determined.

The Guardian lifted its head.

The Hollow had called them.

And they had answered.

1

"The Great Floating Village"

In a hidden corner of the world, tucked deep within an enchanted forest, there existed a magical village named Veraqua. Unlike any ordinary village, Veraqua floated high above the ground, supported by nothing but a curious combination of ancient magic, the giggling winds, and a group of very persistent ducks who refused to ever leave. These ducks, called the Quacks of Veraqua, held an ancient secret: they could flap their wings just right to keep the village afloat.

The villagers of Veraqua were an odd bunch, known for their eccentricities. They lived in treehouses made of shimmering crystal and wore hats made of clouds. They had no need for roads because they simply floated from one house to another by grabbing onto the nearest gust of wind. The most peculiar thing about Veraqua was that nothing stayed in one place—not the houses, not the shops, not even the villagers' socks.

One sunny day, a young and curious villager named Lottie noticed something strange. The village, which usually bobbed gently in the sky like a balloon tied to a string, had begun to drift lower and lower. At first, she thought it was just a strong breeze, but soon the village was only a few feet above the ground. This had never happened before. The Quacks of Veraqua were in complete panic, flapping their wings with all their might, but the village was still sinking!

"Help!" cried Lottie, running through the village square. "The village is falling!"

"Falling?" shouted Mr. Hoot, the owl who ran the only noodle shop in town. He was wearing his signature apron that read "Noodle Queen", even though he was clearly a king. "Nonsense, my dear! I've never heard of a floating village falling! That's just impossible!"

But it was happening.

Lottie quickly gathered her friends: Jasper, the talking rabbit who loved to invent things, and Penny, a mischievous squirrel who had a talent for making gadgets out of anything she found lying around. They decided they had to solve the mystery of why Veraqua was slowly sinking.

"Maybe the ducks are tired," suggested Penny. "I mean, have you seen the size of their wings? They flap a lot.

Maybe they just need a break."

"Maybe," said Jasper, adjusting his oversized glasses. "But I think it has something to do with the Great Floating Stone."

"The Great Floating Stone?" Lottie asked, blinking. "What's that?"

"Nobody knows," said Jasper, "but it's an ancient legend passed down through generations. The stone is what keeps the village afloat. Every hundred years, it needs to be refueled with the power of laughter. If not, the village starts sinking until it disappears completely!"

Lottie gasped. "But we need to make everyone laugh! Quickly!"

With no time to lose, the trio went to work. They tried everything—juggling watermelons, singing ridiculous songs about spaghetti, even performing acrobatics with rubber chickens. But nothing seemed to work. The village was still sinking.

Just when things were looking grim, Penny had a brilliant idea. She grabbed a huge bag of candy and ran to the Quacks of Veraqua. "What do ducks love more than anything?" she asked.

"Cheese!" quacked one of the ducks, though they had no idea why they said it. Another duck shouted, "Watermelon!"

Penny shook her head. "Laughter! You ducks need to make the villagers laugh!"

With a flap of their wings, the Quacks of Veraqua began to perform their most ridiculous dance, waddling and flapping with no care in the world. They sang in quacks, did somersaults mid-air, and honestly looked completely ridiculous.

The villagers, who had never seen such a spectacle, began to laugh—loudly and without restraint. The air was filled with joy and giggles. Lottie, Jasper, and Penny joined in the laughter, as did the whole village. Even the trees seemed to laugh, shaking their leaves like they were in on the joke.

As the laughter filled the air, something magical happened. The village began to rise again, floating higher and higher, until it was back to its original height in the sky.

And there, on the highest tower of Veraqua, the Great Floating Stone began to glow with a warm, golden light. It was now refueled, ready to keep the village floating for another century.

The villagers cheered and celebrated, giving the Quacks of Veraqua a standing ovation. From that day on, the villagers knew that whenever the village started sinking, all they needed was a good laugh—and maybe a dancing duck or two.

2

“The Quest for the Laughing Stone”

The village was quiet now, but only because the villagers had temporarily paused their panicked chatter. Lottie, Jasper, and Penny stood at the edge of the floating square, looking at the Great Floating Stone that now glowed faintly, as though waiting for something to happen.

“I still can’t believe the village was actually sinking,” Lottie muttered, rubbing her head. "What if it happens again?"

“We’ll figure it out,” Jasper said, adjusting his glasses and pulling out a tiny notepad filled with scribbles. “I’m sure the key is hidden somewhere in the village. The Great Floating Stone has to be connected to something ancient. Maybe it’s the ducks—those funny ducks have been around forever.”

"Or maybe it's the candy," Penny said, her tail flicking eagerly. "Candy makes everything better, right? We should bring a big bag to the stone. Maybe it just needs a little sugar!"

Before Lottie could respond, a loud flap echoed through the village, followed by a stream of loud quacking. The Quacks of Veraqua had gathered again—this time in a circle, flapping their wings in unison and performing what could only be described as the world's most confusing dance.

"This is no time for dance!" shouted Mr. Hoot, the owl who ran the noodle shop. "We need a solution! The village can't survive on laughter alone!"

"Oh, but it can!" cried Lottie, feeling more confident now. "Laughter's the key, right? But we need a special kind of laughter—the kind that comes from the heart. Not just silly jokes or funny dances. I think we need to take the laughter somewhere else."

Penny blinked. "Somewhere else? Like... a comedy club?"

"No," Lottie said, thinking hard. "What if we have to find the true source of the village's joy? Something ancient that's been forgotten. We have to go beyond what we know!"

Jasper quickly scribbled down a note. "Ancient source... forgotten joy..." he muttered. "I have an idea!"

"I think I know where we need to go," Penny said with a mischievous grin. "There's a place deep in the forest. The Laughing Hollow. No one talks about it much, but legend says it's where all the laughter in Veraqua comes from. If we can find it, we might discover how to refuel the Great Floating Stone."

Lottie's eyes widened. "You've heard of it?"

"Well," Penny shrugged, "I've seen it, but I've never dared to go inside. They say there are enchanted mirrors that laugh at you, and trees that play pranks. It's... a bit unpredictable."

"Perfect!" said Lottie, grinning. "That sounds like just the kind of place we need."

And so, the trio set off, marching bravely into the heart of Elderwood Forest. The deeper they went, the stranger the trees seemed to get. They twisted and bent in odd directions, like they were trying to tell jokes

with their branches.

"I think we're getting closer," Jasper whispered, looking at a tree that was juggling acorns. "The laughter here is definitely... different."

After a few more twists and turns, they arrived at the Laughing Hollow. It was a wide clearing, with trees that bent into curious shapes, their trunks hollowed out like giant laughing mouths. The ground was soft and squishy, almost like it was giggling beneath their feet.

"You're sure this is the place?" Penny asked nervously, her tail twitching.

Lottie nodded. "It feels right. Let's go in."

As they entered the hollow, the air seemed to hum with energy. Suddenly, a loud cackle echoed through the trees.

"Who dares enter the Laughing Hollow?!" came a booming voice. From nowhere, a giant, glowing mirror appeared in front of them. It was so big that it covered the entire sky, reflecting everything back at them in a thousand distorted versions.

"I dare!" Lottie called back, her voice steady. "We need your help! The village of Veraqua is sinking, and we need to find the source of true laughter to save it!"

The mirror laughed again, louder this time. "Oh, you want the source of laughter? I am the source of laughter! But before I help you, you must solve a riddle."

"Oh no," muttered Penny. "Not another riddle."

"No time for riddles!" Jasper grumbled, but Lottie held up a hand.

"It's okay. We'll solve it. What's the riddle?"

The mirror smiled mischievously. "What is invisible and makes the world smile, but only those who truly believe can hear its sound?"

The three friends stared at each other, thinking hard.

"Come on, think!" Lottie urged. "It has to be something funny but also magical..."

And then it hit her. "Laughter! It's laughter! The sound of true laughter is invisible, but it can make the world smile!"

The mirror glowed brighter. "You are correct! You may now enter the heart of the Laughing Hollow. But beware—the laughter here can be overwhelming. It will test you, make you giggle until you can't stop. But only those who can control their laughter will find the answer."

The mirror vanished, and a doorway appeared in its place. The trio exchanged nervous glances.

"We've come this far," Lottie said. "Let's see what happens."

With that, they stepped into the heart of the Laughing Hollow, ready for whatever strange and funny challenges awaited them.

3

"The Laughing Hollow"

The forest was alive with the sounds of rustling leaves and distant birdcalls as Lottie, Jasper, and Penny ventured deeper into the heart of Elderwood Forest. The air had a strange, almost electric feel to it, buzzing with magic that the villagers of Veraqua were only beginning to understand.

Lottie pushed aside a branch, revealing the entrance to a wide, open clearing. The trees around them twisted and bent at odd angles, their trunks forming strange shapes, like contorted faces frozen mid-laugh. The ground beneath their feet was soft and spongy, as if the very earth was giggling.

"This is it," Penny whispered. "The Laughing Hollow."

The clearing before them was breathtaking—and baffling. Giant trees bent at impossible angles, their branches arching above to form a twisted canopy. From the trees hung what appeared to be hundreds of laughing faces, some smiling widely, others caught in mid-laugh. Their eyes twinkled with mischief, and their mouths opened and closed as if they were echoing the sounds of joy.

A low chuckle echoed through the Hollow, sending a shiver down Lottie's spine.

"I feel like we're being watched," Lottie said nervously. "Are we sure this is the right place?"

"You're not just being watched," Penny replied with a mischievous grin. "You're being tested."

Suddenly, a booming voice rang out from nowhere, making the ground beneath them rumble.

"Who dares enter the Laughing Hollow?"

Lottie jumped, her heart racing. The voice seemed to come from all directions, like the entire forest itself was speaking. "We—we come in search of the source of laughter," she stammered. "Our village is sinking, and we need the power of true laughter to keep it afloat."

The laughing faces in the trees seemed to shift and twist as the voice responded, "You seek the power of the Great Floating Stone, but first, you must prove yourselves worthy. Solve my riddle, and I shall grant you passage. Fail, and the Hollow will trap you forever in its laughter."

Lottie exchanged a glance with her friends. "We don't have much choice. What's the riddle?"

The voice boomed again, this time accompanied by the sound of laughter so contagious that even the trees seemed to chuckle along.

"Listen carefully," the voice said. "What is invisible and makes the world smile, but only those who truly believe can hear its sound?"

The trio stood frozen. The riddle echoed in their minds, bouncing between them like a bouncing ball of confusion.

"I know this one!" Jasper suddenly exclaimed, eyes wide with realization. "It's laughter! Laughter is invisible, and it makes everyone smile. It's what we need to save the village!"

Lottie's face lit up. "That's it! We need to answer with laughter, not just words."

"Laughter?" Penny asked, eyeing the Hollow warily. "But how are we supposed to make the forest laugh?"

The voice chuckled again, this time with what sounded like a hint of approval. "You have the answer, but the true test remains. You must make me laugh, not with your words, but with the purest form of joy."

Suddenly, the air around them shifted. The laughing faces in the trees grinned wider, and the ground trembled with mirth. The trees began to sway, their branches twisting as if they were preparing to perform some kind of dance.

Lottie looked around, trying to think of a way to summon that pure joy. The magical energy of the Hollow felt so heavy, so powerful—how could they make it laugh?

Jasper stepped forward, pulling out a small, peculiar device he had been tinkering with earlier—a device that looked like a cross between a kazoo and a rubber chicken. "Maybe this will work!" he said with a grin. "You never know what might set things off!"

He blew into the kazoo-chicken hybrid, producing a sound that was part honk, part squawk. The Hollow fell silent. For a moment, it seemed as though nothing would happen. But then, a deep rumbling laughter erupted from the trees. It wasn't just any laugh—it was a belly laugh, the kind that made you feel warm and full of joy. The trees shook with laughter, their branches bouncing up and down in rhythm.

Lottie and Penny stared in disbelief. "That worked?" Penny asked, wide-eyed.

Before anyone could answer, the voice returned, still chuckling in the background.

"Clever," it said. "But that was only the beginning. To gain passage, you must now perform a task that requires true laughter. You must entertain the forest—not with tricks, but with joy in your hearts."

Lottie's heart skipped a beat. "How do we do that?"

The voice chuckled again. "You will see."

At that moment, the ground around them split open, revealing a hidden path that led deeper into the Hollow. The path seemed to be alive, wriggling and twisting as though it were full of giggles. On either side, the trees continued to sway, their leaves dancing with joy.

“Looks like we’re going in,” Lottie said, taking a deep breath. “Let’s stick together.”

With that, the trio ventured into the Laughing Hollow, not knowing what lay ahead but determined to solve the mystery and save their village.

As they walked, the trees seemed to follow them, their faces lighting up with laughter. It was as if they were cheering them on, encouraging them to continue. The air was thick with magical energy, and everywhere they looked, there were strange, whimsical creatures hiding in the shadows—mischievous squirrels that giggled like children, rabbits with painted faces, and even flowers that bloomed with laughter.

“This place is... something else,” Penny said, eyes wide with wonder. “It’s like the forest lives off of laughter.”

“Exactly,” Lottie said, suddenly understanding. “The forest is a reflection of what Veraqua needs—the true, pure joy that comes from within. And we need to find that, too.”

They pressed forward, each step echoing with the sound of laughter that surrounded them, as the mysteries of the Laughing Hollow continued to unfold.

4

"The Laughter Trials Begin"

The path they followed through the Laughing Hollow grew narrower, with trees bending closer and closer, their branches twisting and tangling like giant fingers reaching out. The ground beneath their feet seemed to giggle softly, shifting as they walked, making their steps feel like they were walking on clouds. It was as though the forest itself was watching, waiting for their next move.

"Okay, that was easy enough," Penny said, adjusting her tail as they walked. "But I've got a feeling this is just the beginning."

"You're right," Lottie said, looking ahead with determination. "We've passed the first test. But the Laughing Hollow doesn't give up that easily. There's more we have to do if we're going to save Veraqua."

Jasper pulled out his trusty notepad and jotted down a few calculations. "It's all about balance," he muttered to himself. "The village is floating because of laughter. If we can just find a way to harness it, maybe we can use it to power the Great Floating Stone."

Just then, the forest seemed to grow even quieter. The trees stopped their playful swaying, and the giggles in the ground faded into a soft, expectant hum. The air felt charged with anticipation.

Lottie froze. "Did anyone else feel that?"

Before anyone could answer, the laughter stopped completely, and a new voice—this time soft and teasing—rang out from all directions.

"Welcome to the first trial, dear travelers," the voice said, its tone lilting like a song. "You wish to save your village, but first, you must prove that your hearts are full of true laughter. Only then will you be worthy of the Great Floating Stone's power."

The trees parted to reveal a wide, open area. In the center was a large, circular stage made of soft moss, with flowers blooming in spirals around it. On the stage stood a strange creature—half rabbit, half jester—dressed in bright, patchwork clothing. It had a painted smile that stretched from ear to ear, and its eyes twinkled with mischief.

"Well, well, well," the creature said, hopping forward on one foot. "I am the Jester of the Laughing Hollow, and I'm here to see if you truly understand the nature of funny."

"Fun?" Penny whispered, her ears twitching. "Is this some kind of comedy challenge?"

The Jester laughed, a high-pitched, musical sound. "Not just any comedy, dear one. You must create a spectacle, an uproarious show of true hilarity. Only then will you be allowed to proceed."

Lottie exchanged a look with her friends. "So we have to make this Jester laugh? Seems simple enough."

"Simple?" Jasper raised an eyebrow. "We're talking about a magical trial in a forest full of enchanted laughter. This isn't going to be easy."

"We can do it," Lottie said, grinning. "How hard can it be to make a giant rabbit-jester laugh?"

The Jester clapped his hands, making a sound like a thousand bells ringing. "Then show me what you've got. I shall be your judge. But be warned—if you fail, you will remain trapped here, caught in endless laughter!"

Lottie took a deep breath and stepped forward. She wasn't sure where to start, but she was determined to give it her best shot.

"Alright," she said, trying to keep her voice steady. "Let's start with something simple. A joke!"

She cleared her throat. "Why don't skeletons fight each other?"

The Jester raised an eyebrow, clearly not amused. "Why?"

"Because they don't have the guts!" Lottie exclaimed, throwing her arms wide.

The Jester stared at her blankly for a moment, and then, to Lottie's surprise, he didn't laugh. Instead, he sighed and shook his head.

"Not quite," he said, waving his hand dismissively. "That was an easy one. Let's see what else you've got."

Penny stepped up next, her tail flicking nervously behind her. "Okay, how about this?"

She performed a quick somersault, landing in a perfect split. "What do you get when you cross a squirrel with a trampoline?"

The Jester blinked, intrigued but still not laughing. "I don't know. What?"

"A wild, bouncy nut!" Penny said, throwing her hands up in triumph.

The Jester smiled faintly but still didn't laugh. "Cute, but still not quite enough. You're getting warmer, though."

Jasper stepped forward, his brow furrowed in concentration. "Alright, let's see. If humor is what you want, I've got a scientific approach."

He pulled out a small gadget and pressed a button. A little robot squirrel popped out, wearing glasses and a bowtie. "Allow me to introduce Professor Nutty!" Jasper said with flair. The robot squirrel began to perform a series of exaggerated, clumsy dance moves.

The Jester's mouth twitched, but he still didn't laugh.

Lottie groaned. "This is impossible! We're not going to win him over with silly jokes!"

Suddenly, something clicked in Lottie's mind. She remembered something her grandmother had once told her: "True laughter comes from the heart, not from trying too hard to be funny."

"Alright," Lottie said, taking a deep breath. "Maybe we've been doing it wrong. Maybe the trick isn't in the joke itself, but in how we tell it."

She turned to Penny and Jasper. "Let's try something different. Something that's just us."

The two friends nodded, and Lottie stepped back.

"I've got an idea," Penny said. "Jasper, remember that time we got trapped in the giant mud puddle? We were covered in slime, and the ducks wouldn't stop laughing?"

Jasper laughed. "I remember! I swore I'd never laugh at a puddle again!"

"Well, you know what?" Penny grinned. "That's exactly the kind of thing we need. Real moments, real laughter."

Together, they began to tell the story of their adventure with the mud puddle, exaggerating the details for comedic effect. Lottie remembered how they had all slipped and slid around, covered in mud, trying to escape the quacking ducks. The more they laughed about it, the more the Jester seemed to smile, his painted grin widening.

Finally, Penny mimicked the ducks' laughter in a way that was so absurd, so perfectly timed, that it was impossible not to laugh. The Jester's eyes sparkled with mirth, and before anyone knew it, he was laughing—really laughing—his voice echoing through the Hollow like the sound of a thousand joyful bells.

"You've got it!" the Jester exclaimed, doubling over with laughter. "That's what I wanted to see! True laughter, from the heart! Well done!"

Lottie, Penny, and Jasper stood there, beaming. They had passed the first trial, not through jokes or tricks, but by embracing the pure joy of being themselves.

"Well done, travelers!" the Jester said, his laughter finally subsiding. "You may proceed. But remember—true laughter is the most powerful magic of all. Hold onto that, and you'll go far."

With a flourish, the Jester disappeared into thin air, and the path ahead of them opened wide.

Lottie, Penny, and Jasper exchanged high-fives. "That wasn't so bad," Penny said, still chuckling.

"We've got this," Lottie said, grinning. "Let's save Veraqua."

And with that, they continued deeper into the Laughing Hollow, ready for whatever trials lay ahead.

5

"The Tickling Trees"

The Laughing Hollow seemed to grow more and more mischievous as they ventured deeper into its heart. The laughter-filled air thickened with magic, and the trees, once playful and charming, now took on a more active role in the trials that lay ahead. The ground beneath their feet was springy, as if the earth itself had a sense of humor and couldn't help but giggle every time they took a step.

"I've got a bad feeling about this," Penny said, twitching her ears nervously. "I'm starting to feel like the forest is... playing with us."

"Playing with us?" Jasper said, looking around cautiously. "More like pranking us."

Lottie nodded, keeping her eyes peeled for anything suspicious. "We need to stay focused. The last trial was about finding real joy, but something tells me this one's going to be trickier."

As they walked, the trees around them seemed to hum with laughter, their branches swaying and bending, as though they were setting up some grand, invisible performance. At first, it felt like the breeze was carrying the sound of birds singing, but as they went further, the sound shifted into something more... playful.

Suddenly, one of the trees—a tall, thin pine with shimmering, green leaves—snapped to attention and tilted its head toward them. A low chuckle echoed from its trunk. Before Lottie could react, its bark split open with a giggle and a pair of long, spindly branches shot out like tickling fingers, sweeping toward them.

"Watch out!" Lottie shouted, diving out of the way as the branches whooshed past.

Penny yelped, dodging just in time as one of the branches brushed past her tail. "What in the world was that?!"

"I think it was a tickling tree," Jasper said, stepping back, his eyes wide. "These trees... they're not just alive. They're mischievous. They're actively trying to make us laugh!"

Before they could catch their breath, more trees joined in. One by one, tall oak trees with wide, leafy branches swiveled toward them, their bark cracking into smiles, and soon, dozens of trees were giggling in unison. The air was filled with the sound of playful cackles, and long, twisting vines dropped from the branches like ropes, swaying with ticklish energy.

"Ha! Gotcha!" one tree's voice called, as a vine swept beneath Penny's feet. She jumped, laughing despite herself. "You can't escape the tickles!"

"I think it's safe to say we're in the tickling part of the trial," Lottie said, breathless from dodging a particularly aggressive branch. "They're not going to stop until we laugh."

"Yeah, but I don't think just laughing will get us out of this," Penny said, narrowly avoiding another vine. "These trees are tickling us! We need to figure out how to deal with this—without just giggling the whole way through!"

Jasper's eyes glimmered with thought. "Wait, maybe this is a test of control. These trees want us to lose our composure. They want to see if we can resist the urge to laugh."

"I can't resist," Penny said, clutching her sides as a vine swished beneath her again. "I'm trying not to laugh, but it's just too ticklish!"

Lottie glanced around at the trees, their faces now all twisted in gleeful delight, their trunks bobbing with laughter. She noticed something strange, though. The tickling vines that whipped around them were quick to move, but their timing was off. The trees were trying to get a reaction, but they couldn't seem to land their tickles at the right moment.

"It's like they're waiting for us to react," Lottie said, eyes narrowing. "But the real test isn't just about resisting laughter. It's about staying calm, no matter how ticklish this gets."

"Exactly!" Jasper said, grinning. "It's a test of control! We have to stay in control and laugh on our terms, not theirs!"

A vine darted for Lottie's arm, but she managed to pull it back just in time. "We need to take control of the laughter—we need to decide when to laugh, not let the trees push us into it."

The trio huddled together, eyes focused as more vines whipped around them, causing them to giggle every time they brushed against their sides or tails.

"Alright," Lottie said, her voice firm. "When the trees want to tickle, we need to show them we can laugh when we choose. Let's do it together."

Penny nodded, trying to steady her breath. "On three?"

"One... two... three!" the three of them said in unison.

And with that, the trio let out a burst of genuine laughter—a hearty, joyful laugh that rang out across the Hollow. It wasn't forced, and it wasn't because of the tickling vines. They were laughing because they wanted to, and the trees could feel it.

The tickling vines hesitated for a moment, as if unsure how to respond. The air seemed to pause, and the sound of rustling leaves quieted. Then, with a sudden whoosh, the vines stopped moving entirely, and the trees stopped their incessant giggling. The laughter from the forest echoed into a deep, satisfied hum.

"Well done!" a voice rang out from the trees, as the tickling vines slowly retracted back into the branches. "You've passed the second trial. You've shown that you can control the magic of laughter. But be warned, not all laughter is as harmless as it seems."

The trees began to sway once more, but this time, the laughter wasn't as sinister. It was playful, and the air felt lighter. The trial was over—but the message had been clear. The Laughing Hollow was a place of chaos and magic, where control and composure mattered just as much as joy and laughter.

The path ahead opened up, the tickling trees bowing as if to acknowledge their victory.

"That was intense," Penny said, wiping a tear from her eye. "I never thought I'd be tickled into a trial."

"I guess we've got a lot to learn about how laughter works here," Lottie said, grinning. "But we're getting better at it."

Jasper adjusted his glasses and looked ahead. "On to the next trial, I suppose. Whatever that may be."

As they moved forward, the giggles of the trees slowly faded behind them. But one thing was certain: in the Laughing Hollow, no trial was ever quite what it seemed. And no matter how tricky the challenge, they would face it together—with laughter and a little bit of control.

6

"The River of Echoes"

The trio pressed onward, leaving the Tickling Trees behind. The air grew cooler as the path led them to a serene, glimmering river that sparkled under the sunlight. Unlike the mischievous trees, the river seemed calm and inviting, its surface smooth like glass. However, the magical energy emanating from it was unmistakable.

"What is this place?" Lottie whispered, kneeling at the riverbank. The water reflected her face perfectly, but something about it felt off.

Penny's ears twitched. "This doesn't feel like a normal river. It's... too quiet."

Jasper tapped his chin, observing the still water. "If the Laughing Hollow has taught us anything so far, it's that nothing here is as it seems. Be careful."

Lottie dipped her finger into the river, causing ripples to spread outward. As they did, a soft chuckling sound began to echo, growing louder with each wave. The trio jumped back, startled, as the water began to shimmer and rise, forming humanoid shapes made entirely of liquid.

The figures stood tall, their laughter echoing eerily. Each one resembled a distorted reflection of Lottie, Penny, and Jasper, as if the river had copied their images but twisted them into something slightly off-kilter.

“Welcome to the River of Echoes,” the watery version of Lottie said, her voice a strange mix of laughter and calm. “You have passed the trials of joy and control, but now you must face yourselves.”

“Face ourselves?” Penny asked, narrowing her eyes. “What does that mean?”

The watery Jasper stepped forward, his liquid form rippling as he moved. “The laughter you seek must come from knowing who you truly are. We are your echoes, your reflections. Only by accepting us will you be allowed to cross the river.”

The real Jasper adjusted his glasses nervously. "This feels... ominous."

The watery Penny giggled, her form dancing across the riverbank. "Oh, it's nothing ominous. It's just a little fun! But beware—if you deny us or fight us, the river will pull you in, and you'll become part of it forever."

"That's not fun!" Penny exclaimed, taking a step back.

Lottie held up her hand. "Wait. Let's think about this. They're reflections of us, right? Maybe this is about confronting our flaws or insecurities."

The watery Lottie smirked. "Exactly, brave leader. Let's see if you can handle what you find."

The reflections stepped closer, and the trio realized they couldn't just ignore them. The reflections seemed to mirror not only their physical forms but their thoughts and emotions, exposing feelings they hadn't fully acknowledged.

Lottie's Trial
The watery Lottie circled her, grinning slyly. "You act

so strong, but deep down, you're afraid. You're scared of failing your village, aren't you? What if you're not the leader they think you are?"

Lottie clenched her fists, her heart pounding. It was true—she'd been carrying the weight of the entire village's survival on her shoulders, and doubt often crept in. But she took a deep breath and spoke firmly.

"Yes, I'm scared. But being brave doesn't mean not being afraid—it means acting despite the fear. I don't have all the answers, but I won't give up."

The watery Lottie smiled and dissolved back into the river. "Well done."

Penny's Trial

The watery Penny darted around her, laughing mockingly. "You think you're funny, but you're always hiding behind jokes. Do you really think you're good enough to help save the village? Or are you just a sidekick?"

Penny's ears drooped, and for a moment, she didn't know what to say. She had always used humor to deflect serious situations, afraid that she wasn't as important as Lottie or Jasper. But then she thought about everything they had faced together.

"I might not be the smartest or the bravest," Penny said, her voice steady, "but I know my worth. My jokes make people happy, and that's just as important as anything else."

The watery Penny chuckled softly, then melted into the river. "Nicely done."

Jasper's Trial

The watery Jasper stood still, staring at him with piercing eyes. "You rely on logic and gadgets, but what about your heart? You keep your feelings bottled up, afraid they'll make you weak. Are you just hiding behind your inventions?"

Jasper adjusted his glasses, feeling exposed. It was true—he often used science as a shield, afraid to express his emotions. But as he looked at Lottie and Penny, he realized that his friends valued him for who he was, not just his intellect.

"I might not wear my heart on my sleeve," Jasper said, his voice firm, "but that doesn't mean I don't care. My inventions are my way of protecting the people I love."

The watery Jasper nodded and dissolved into the river. "You've learned well."

As the final echo disappeared, the river's surface shimmered and stilled. The laughter grew softer, fading into a peaceful hum. A stone bridge emerged from the water, leading to the other side.

"You did it," Penny said, her voice filled with relief. "We faced our reflections and didn't get pulled in."

Lottie smiled. "We didn't just face them. We accepted them. That's what this trial was about."

Jasper adjusted his glasses and took the first step onto the bridge. "Then let's keep moving. We're one step closer to saving Veraqua."

As they crossed the bridge, the River of Echoes sparkled behind them, a reminder of the importance of self-awareness and acceptance. The path ahead seemed brighter, but the Laughing Hollow still held more trials—and more mysteries.

7

"The Gigglevine Labyrinth"

As the trio crossed the stone bridge, the air grew warmer, carrying a faint, sugary scent. Lush greenery stretched before them, and the trail led to a massive archway woven from thick, vibrant vines that shimmered with a faint golden hue. Lottie, Penny, and Jasper paused to take in the sight, but their moment of awe quickly faded as the vines moved, curling and twisting like living creatures.

"What do you think this is?" Penny asked, her nose twitching at the sweet scent. "It smells like candy, but it's definitely... alive."

Jasper peered at the vines, adjusting his glasses. "It's some sort of magical plant. But why does it feel so... playful?"

Suddenly, the archway parted, revealing a labyrinth beyond it, the walls formed entirely of the same golden vines. A deep, booming laugh echoed through the air, startling them.

"Welcome to the Gigglevine Labyrinth!" a disembodied voice announced, cheerful and grand. "To proceed, you must navigate the maze of laughter. But beware—these vines love to play tricks!"

Before they could respond, the archway behind them closed, leaving them no choice but to enter the maze. The vines shimmered and rustled, giggling softly as if anticipating the chaos to come.

The First Path: Penny's Antics
Penny led the way, her tail swishing nervously as they moved through the winding paths. The sweet scent grew stronger, and every so often, a golden vine would dart out to tickle her nose, making her sneeze.

"Okay, this isn't funny anymore!" Penny said, waving her paws to fend off another tickling vine.

But the vines didn't stop. They danced and twirled, brushing against her fur and tugging at her tail. Finally, fed up, Penny burst into exaggerated giggles. "Alright, alright, you win! It's funny, okay?"

To everyone's surprise, as Penny laughed, the vines relaxed, parting to reveal the next path.

Jasper raised an eyebrow. "It seems the vines respond to genuine laughter. That must be the key."

"Great," Penny said, still chuckling. "At least I'm good at laughing."

The Second Path: Jasper's Logic
As they moved deeper into the maze, they came across a section where the walls pulsated with faint, golden light. A low, melodic hum filled the air, and the vines rearranged themselves, forming intricate patterns that shifted like a puzzle.

Jasper stepped forward, studying the patterns carefully. "This looks like a logic game," he said, his voice steady. "If we align the vines correctly, it should unlock the next path."

The vines seemed to giggle in response, as if taunting him. Jasper frowned but began shifting and tugging at the vines, trying to decipher their playful logic. Each time he moved one, the others rearranged themselves, often in nonsensical ways.

"You're overthinking it!" Penny teased, still amused from her earlier encounter.

Jasper sighed but decided to approach the puzzle differently. Instead of relying solely on logic, he let himself relax, treating the puzzle like a game. With this lighter mindset, the vines finally aligned, and the path opened.

Jasper smirked. "Sometimes, thinking like a child helps."

The Third Path: Lottie's Leadership
The final section of the labyrinth brought them to a large, circular clearing. A single, massive vine rose from the ground, writhing and cackling. It formed a twisting staircase that led to a glowing exit above.

“Climbing that thing?” Penny asked, wide-eyed. “It’s moving! How are we supposed to do that?”

The disembodied voice returned, booming with laughter. “The leader must guide the climb! Only teamwork will see you through.”

Lottie nodded, understanding the challenge. The staircase was erratic, swaying and shifting unpredictably, but she had to keep her friends calm and focused.

“Alright,” Lottie said, her voice steady. “Jasper, you analyze the movements and tell us when to step. Penny, you keep the mood light—make us laugh if things get tense. I’ll lead the way and keep us steady.”

With Lottie’s guidance, Jasper’s observations, and Penny’s jokes, the trio ascended the wobbly staircase, laughing through the chaos. Each time they stumbled, the vines seemed to cheer them on, as if enjoying their determination.

Finally, they reached the glowing exit, and as they stepped through, the vines released a triumphant cheer before retreating.

A New Ally

On the other side of the labyrinth, they found themselves in a small, sunlit clearing. A small, fox-like creature with golden fur and twinkling eyes waited for them. It wore a tiny jester's hat and carried a staff adorned with a crystal that shimmered with laughter.

"Congratulations!" the creature said, bowing dramatically. "I am Gigglesworth, guardian of the labyrinth. You've proven yourselves worthy of continuing your journey!"

"Another talking animal?" Penny muttered, rolling her eyes. "We're collecting these like souvenirs."

Gigglesworth ignored her and continued, "The laughter trials will only grow harder, but I see great potential in you. Take this." He handed them the staff. "This will help you harness the magic of joy when the time comes. Use it wisely!"

With that, Gigglesworth vanished in a swirl of golden light, leaving them alone in the clearing. The trio stared at the staff, its crystal glowing softly.

"We're getting closer," Lottie said, holding the staff. "But I have a feeling the hardest part is yet to come."

"Great," Penny said, yawning. "I hope the next trial doesn't involve more tickling."

With the staff in hand and new determination, the trio moved forward, ready to face whatever the Laughing Hollow threw at them next.

8

"The Chorus of Shadows"

The trio pressed on from the clearing, holding the magical staff given by Gigglesworth. The forest ahead felt different—darker, quieter, and heavier. The once-cheerful atmosphere of the Laughing Hollow was replaced by an eerie stillness. Lottie gripped the staff tightly, Penny's ears twitched nervously, and even Jasper seemed more subdued than usual.

"What is this place?" Penny whispered, glancing around. The towering trees cast long, shifting shadows across the ground, making it hard to tell where they were heading.

Jasper adjusted his glasses, observing their surroundings. "This must be another trial, but it feels... different. Less playful, more—"

"Sinister," Lottie finished, her voice steady but cautious. "Stay close. This might be a test of a different kind."

As they moved forward, faint whispers began to swirl around them, like fragments of a forgotten song. The whispers grew louder, forming a haunting melody that echoed through the trees. The shadows on the ground started to move, twisting and writhing like living creatures.

"Great," Penny muttered, trying to mask her nervousness. "Creepy singing shadows. Just what we needed."

The Shadow Chorus Appears

The trio entered a clearing where the shadows gathered, forming into humanoid shapes with glowing eyes. They began to hum in unison, creating a mesmerizing but unsettling tune. One shadow stepped forward, its voice deep and resonant.

"Welcome to the Chorus of Shadows," it said. "We are the echoes of fear, doubt, and sorrow. To pass, you must face the laughter within darkness. Can you find joy when surrounded by shadow?"

The challenge was clear: the trio had to bring light and laughter to this gloomy realm. But how?

Jasper's Solution: A Spark of Light

Jasper inspected the magical staff, noticing the crystal faintly glowing in response to the shadows' melody. "This staff reacts to laughter," he said. "Maybe it can channel light if we focus on something joyful."

"Like what?" Penny asked, eyeing the shadows warily. "I'm not exactly brimming with joy right now."

Jasper adjusted his glasses, thinking hard. "Lottie, you're the leader. What's something that always made us laugh back in Veraqua?"

Lottie hesitated, then smiled. "The time Penny fell into the bakery cart and got covered in flour during the harvest festival. She looked like a ghost!"

Penny crossed her arms, but her lips twitched into a grin. "Oh, yeah? What about the time you got stuck in the town fountain trying to rescue a rubber duck?"

Laughter bubbled up between them, and the staff glowed brighter. The shadows recoiled slightly, their song faltering.

"It's working!" Jasper said. "Keep going!"

The Laughter Game
The shadows began to change tactics, swirling around the trio and whispering words of doubt and fear. "You'll fail," they murmured. "The village is doomed. You're not strong enough."

But Lottie, Penny, and Jasper didn't let the voices shake them. Instead, they turned the doubts into a game.

"Fail? Me?" Penny said with mock indignation. "I've been failing at cooking for years, and I'm still here!"

"And I've failed at building inventions plenty of times," Jasper added. "Remember the exploding tea kettle?"

Lottie laughed. "Oh, and let's not forget my epic failure at teaching the village kids how to dance. I ended up tripping over my own feet!"

Their laughter grew louder and more genuine, and the staff began to shine with a radiant golden light. The shadows hissed and shrank, their chorus replaced by silence.

A New Ally Emerges

As the last shadow dissolved, a figure stepped out from the darkness. It was a tall, elegant being made of shimmering light and shadow, its face serene and kind.

“You have succeeded,” it said, its voice melodic. “You’ve proven that laughter is not just for joy but also a weapon against fear. I am Chordis, guardian of the Chorus. You’ve earned my blessing.”

Chordis placed a hand on the staff, and the crystal grew brighter, pulsating with newfound energy. “With this, you may now channel the harmony of light and shadow. Use it wisely in the trials ahead.”

The being bowed and disappeared, leaving the trio standing in the now-bright clearing.

Moving Forward
"That was... intense," Penny said, shaking off the last remnants of fear.

"But we did it," Lottie said, her voice filled with determination. "Each trial is teaching us something new. If we keep working together, we'll save Veraqua."

Jasper nodded, holding the glowing staff. "Let's keep going. The forest isn't done with us yet."

With renewed confidence, they pressed on, ready to face whatever the Laughing Hollow had in store.

9

"The Goblin of Guffaws"

After their encounter with the Chorus of Shadows, the trio continued through the dense forest, their path lit by the glowing staff. The air was lighter now, filled with faint giggles that seemed to float like whispers in the breeze. Penny's ears perked up, and she looked around nervously.

"Does anyone else hear that?" she asked, spinning in place. "It's like the forest is laughing at us."

"Given where we are, I wouldn't be surprised," Jasper muttered, tightening his grip on the staff. "But it's definitely getting louder."

Lottie held up a hand, signaling for them to stop. The giggles turned into belly laughter, echoing through the trees. Suddenly, the ground beneath them trembled, and with a loud pop, a figure shot up from the earth like a spring-loaded jack-in-the-box.

Before them stood a small, green-skinned goblin with wild, frizzy orange hair and a grin so wide it looked like it might stretch off his face. He wore a patchwork suit of mismatched colors and a pair of oversized boots that squeaked whenever he moved.

"Welcome, travelers!" the goblin exclaimed, his voice high-pitched and jubilant. "I am Guffwin, the Goblin of Guffaws, master of jokes and jests! If you wish to pass through my domain, you must prove yourselves worthy of my laughter!"

Penny raised an eyebrow. "Let me guess—another trial?"

Guffwin nodded enthusiastically, his hair bouncing. "Oh, but this one's the best yet! To win, you must outwit me in a battle of humor! The rules are simple: make me laugh three times, and I'll let you go. But beware! If your jokes are dull, you'll be trapped here forever in my Hall of Bad Puns!"

The Battle of Humor Begins

The trio exchanged nervous glances. Making a magical goblin laugh sounded easy enough, but the stakes were too high to take lightly. Lottie stepped forward first.

"Alright, Guffwin," she said, standing tall. "Here's one: Why did the scarecrow win an award?"

The goblin tilted his head. "Why?"

"Because he was outstanding in his field!"

Guffwin snorted, his lips twitching, but he quickly composed himself. "Not bad, not bad. But you'll have to do better than that!"

Jasper stepped up next, adjusting his glasses. "I've got one for you. Why don't scientists trust atoms?"

"Why not?" Guffwin asked, leaning forward.

"Because they make up everything."

This time, Guffwin let out a loud chuckle before covering his mouth. "Okay, fine, that's one point. But I'm not easy to break, you know!"

Penny grinned mischievously. "My turn. What do you call a bear with no teeth?"

Guffwin scratched his head. "I don't know. What?"

"A gummy bear!"

The goblin exploded into laughter, falling to the ground and clutching his sides. "Two points! One more, and you win!"

Guffwin's Counterattack

But before they could celebrate, Guffwin sprang back to his feet. "Not so fast! It's my turn now. If I can make you laugh, I get a point too!"

He pulled out a rubber chicken and wiggled it in front of them, making ridiculous faces. Penny stifled a giggle, Jasper rolled his eyes, and Lottie crossed her arms, determined not to crack.

"Hmm, tough crowd," Guffwin muttered, tapping his chin. He suddenly launched into an exaggerated impression of Jasper, complete with fake glasses and a squeaky voice. "Oh, look at me! I'm Jasper, and I love logic! I've calculated the exact probability of this joke working, and it's zero!"

Penny burst out laughing, unable to hold it in. Guffwin grinned triumphantly. "That's one point for me!"

The Final Round

The score was tied, and tension filled the air. Lottie stepped forward again, determined to win. "Alright, Guffwin. Here's my final joke. What do you call cheese that isn't yours?"

The goblin tilted his head, intrigued. "What?"

"Nacho cheese!"

Guffwin froze, his eyes wide. Then he let out an uncontrollable roar of laughter, rolling on the ground and pounding his fists. "That's it! That's the one! You win!"

The Prize

As Guffwin regained his composure, he wiped tears from his eyes and stood up, bowing deeply. "Well done, travelers. You've bested me in the art of humor. For that, you deserve a reward."

With a snap of his fingers, a small golden bell appeared in his hand. He handed it to Lottie.

"This is the Bell of Guffaws," he explained. "Ring it in moments of despair, and it will summon a burst of laughter strong enough to brighten even the darkest day. Use it wisely."

Lottie took the bell and nodded. "Thank you, Guffwin. We'll use it well."

The goblin gave them a wink and disappeared in a puff of smoke, leaving behind the faint sound of giggles.

Moving Forward

The trio walked away from Guffwin's domain, the magical bell safely tucked in Lottie's bag.

"That was surprisingly fun," Penny said, still smiling. "Though I'm glad we didn't end up in the Hall of Bad Puns."

Jasper smirked. "Let's hope the next trial doesn't involve shadow puppets or knock-knock jokes."

Lottie laughed. "Whatever's ahead, we'll face it together. One laugh at a time."

With their spirits lifted, the trio ventured deeper into the Laughing Hollow, the sound of their laughter mingling with the forest's magic.

10

"The Whispering Willows"

As the trio ventured deeper into the Laughing Hollow, the cheerful giggles of Guffwin's domain faded, replaced by a soft rustling sound that seemed to follow their every step. The forest grew denser, the trees taller and older, their bark gnarled and covered in glowing moss. The atmosphere became strangely tranquil, yet unnervingly alive.

"This place feels... different," Jasper said, adjusting his glasses as he examined the towering trees around them.

"Yeah," Penny added, her nose twitching. "It's too quiet. Like the calm before the storm."

Lottie held the Bell of Guffaws tightly in her hand, its golden surface warm to the touch. "Stay close," she said. "Whatever this is, it's another test."

As they walked, the trees around them seemed to lean in closer, their branches intertwining to form a canopy that blocked out the sunlight. The rustling sound grew louder, and then, faint voices began to whisper from the trees.

The Trees Speak

"Who dares disturb the Whispering Willows?" a soft, feminine voice echoed, blending with the wind.

Lottie stopped in her tracks, her eyes scanning the forest. "We're just passing through," she said. "We mean no harm."

The trees groaned as if responding to her words. Another voice, deeper and more ancient, replied, "Passing through is not so simple. The Willows guard the path of memories. To proceed, you must face your pasts."

Penny gulped. "Our... pasts? Can't we just skip this one?"

The voices ignored her. The trees' bark shimmered, and three large willow trees in front of them parted their branches, revealing doorways that glowed faintly.

"One door for each of you," the feminine voice said. "Enter, and face what lies within. Only those who reconcile with their memories may continue."

The trio exchanged uneasy glances.

"Looks like we don't have a choice," Lottie said, stepping toward the glowing doorway meant for her. "We'll meet back here once we're through."

Lottie's Trial: The Lost Day

Inside her doorway, Lottie found herself in Veraqua, standing in the town square. It was a vivid memory: the day she had forgotten to bring water to the harvest festival, causing a massive delay in the celebration.

She watched her younger self pacing nervously as the villagers murmured their disappointment.

"I was so careless," Lottie said aloud. "I let everyone down."

The scene shifted. The villagers approached her younger self, not with anger, but with encouragement. They helped her fix the mistake, turning the day into a success.

The feminine voice whispered in her ear, "Even leaders stumble. True strength lies in learning from your errors."

Lottie smiled, understanding now. She stepped back through the doorway, her heart lighter.

Penny's Trial: The Forgotten Friend

Penny's doorway led her to a quiet glade where a younger version of herself played with a small fox. It was her childhood friend, Niko, who had left the village years ago.

The scene shifted, showing a tearful goodbye as Niko departed, and Penny turned away, pretending not to care.

"I was so afraid of being vulnerable," Penny said, her voice trembling. "I should've told him how much I'd miss him."

The whispers surrounded her, warm and comforting. "It is never too late to honor your feelings."

The scene dissolved, and Penny returned to the clearing, tears in her eyes but a smile on her face.

Jasper's Trial: The Shattered Invention

Jasper entered his doorway to find himself in his old workshop, surrounded by broken contraptions. He saw his younger self sitting amidst the wreckage of a failed project, muttering words of self-doubt.

"I remember this," Jasper said softly. "I gave up for weeks after this failure."

The scene changed, showing him eventually rebuilding the invention with the help of Lottie and Penny. It wasn't perfect, but it worked.

"You've always had the courage to try again," the whispers told him. "That is what truly matters."

Jasper nodded, feeling a renewed sense of confidence as he stepped back through the doorway.

Reunited

The trio emerged from their doorways at the same time, meeting back in the clearing. The air around them felt lighter, as if the forest itself was pleased with their growth.

"You have faced your pasts with courage," the feminine voice said. "The Willows grant you their blessing."

One of the willow trees extended a branch, dropping a shimmering orb into Lottie's hands.

"This is the Orb of Reflection," the voice explained. "It will reveal the truth hidden in any illusion. Use it wisely."

Lottie held the orb close, feeling its warmth. "Thank you. We'll make good use of it."

The trees parted, revealing a new path ahead. The trio exchanged smiles, their bond stronger than ever as they ventured deeper into the forest.

11

"The Riddle of the Rainbow River"

The trio continued their journey through the Laughing Hollow, feeling a strange sense of excitement mixed with unease. After the Whispering Willows and their trials of facing past mistakes, the air was thick with anticipation. The path seemed to wind and shift, leading them toward something new—but what?

As they ventured deeper into the forest, the trees began to thin out, and a sparkling, vibrant river appeared before them. The water shone in an array of colors—blues, purples, greens, and yellows—creating a mesmerizing rainbow effect. The river stretched far across the landscape, its current rushing fiercely.

"This river looks magical," Lottie said, her voice full of awe. "I've never seen anything like it."

Penny's ears twitched as she watched the water flow. "Yeah, but something feels off. It's too... peaceful. Like there's something hidden beneath the surface."

Jasper nodded thoughtfully. "I agree. It's almost too perfect. Let's be cautious."

The River's Challenge

Just as the trio approached the edge of the river, a deep, echoing voice rose from the water. It was rich and musical, with an undertone of mystery.

"To cross this river, you must answer my riddle," the voice boomed. "Solve it correctly, and you may pass. Fail, and the river shall swallow you whole."

Penny's eyes widened. "Did it just threaten us? I don't like this."

Lottie raised a hand. "Stay calm. We've made it this far. I'm sure we can solve whatever this is."

The water rippled, and from the depths rose a figure—a large, shimmering serpent with scales that reflected every color of the rainbow. Its eyes gleamed with ancient wisdom.

"I am the Serpent of the Rainbow River," the voice continued. "And here is your riddle:

I am not alive, but I grow;
I do not have lungs, but I need air;
I do not have a mouth, but water kills me.
What am I?"

The Riddle Game

The trio stood in silence, each of them deep in thought. Lottie furrowed her brow, clearly working through the possibilities. Penny began to pace, muttering to herself, while Jasper stared at the serpent with intense focus.

"I know this one," Penny said suddenly, her tail flicking with excitement. "It's fire! Fire isn't alive, but it grows. It needs air to burn, and water will extinguish it."

Lottie nodded in agreement. "Fire makes perfect sense. Let's tell the serpent."

With a shared look of determination, Lottie stepped forward. "The answer is fire."

The Serpent's Response

The Serpent of the Rainbow River's eyes gleamed brighter, and it lowered its head in approval. "Correct. You have answered well, travelers. The river will now grant you passage."

With a swift movement, the serpent dove back into the water, and the current slowed. The rainbow glow of the river shifted, creating a beautiful bridge made of shimmering light that extended from one side to the other.

"Cross with care," the serpent's voice echoed from below. "Remember: Knowledge will always light the way, but curiosity may be your greatest ally."

Crossing the River

The trio stepped onto the magical bridge, the soft glow beneath their feet keeping them steady as they crossed. The river below sparkled like a thousand diamonds, and the colors seemed to shift with each step they took. It was as if the river itself was alive with energy, pulsing with magic.

"This is amazing," Jasper whispered, his voice filled with wonder. "It's like walking on a rainbow."

Penny smiled but kept her eyes on the path ahead. "It's beautiful, but it's still a little creepy. Who knows what else this forest has in store?"

Lottie kept her focus, her hand tightly gripping the Bell of Guffaws in case they needed it. "Stay alert. We don't know what's waiting for us on the other side."

A New Discovery

As they crossed the final stretch of the bridge, the light shifted, and a dense fog began to roll in from the other side of the river. The trio stepped off the bridge, finding themselves in a completely different landscape. The fog was thick, swirling around their feet, and the trees here were unlike anything they had seen before. They were tall and twisted, with bark that seemed to shimmer like glass.

Suddenly, they heard a soft, melodic hum in the air—a gentle, almost hypnotic tune that seemed to call them deeper into the fog.

"That's not creepy at all," Penny muttered under her breath, her fur bristling. "What now?"

Lottie scanned the area. "Something's out there, but we'll need to trust each other. We've faced everything together so far."

Jasper nodded, his voice steady. "We'll stay close. Whatever comes, we face it as a team."

The fog swirled around them, and they took their first steps into the unknown, the hum growing louder with each step.

12

"The Melody of Mist"

The fog around them thickened as they ventured further into the mysterious landscape. The soft, hypnotic hum they had heard earlier now surrounded them from all sides, filling the air like an invisible tide. The trio moved cautiously, each step careful and deliberate as they tried to make sense of the shifting mist. The trees loomed tall and twisted, their bark reflecting the faint glow of the river behind them, creating an eerie, otherworldly glow.

"This doesn't feel right," Penny whispered, her ears flicking at the strange sound. "The hum's getting louder. It's almost... it's almost like it's calling us."

Lottie nodded, her expression serious. "I agree. Whatever this is, we have to stay focused. Let's keep moving."

Jasper, adjusting his glasses, glanced around nervously. "I don't like this at all. The fog seems to be following us."

The Source of the Sound

The trio continued walking, trying to ignore the growing feeling of unease that hung in the air like a heavy cloud. After what felt like hours, the fog began to part, revealing an unusual clearing ahead. In the center stood a large, stone archway, its surface covered in intricate carvings. Above it, a faint, glowing symbol hovered in the air, pulsing gently in time with the melody.

The hum grew louder as they approached, and with it, a new sound joined in—a soft, sweet voice, singing in a language none of them recognized.

"This isn't just some random sound," Lottie murmured, her voice full of wonder and caution. "It's a song... and it's coming from the arch."

Penny tilted her head, trying to make sense of the voice. "But it sounds like it's speaking directly to us... like it's talking."

Jasper frowned, looking closely at the glowing symbol above the arch. "It's magic—ancient magic. The carvings on the stone... they tell a story. If we want to understand what's going on, we need to solve it."

The Song's Puzzle

As they approached the arch, the melodic voice began to shift. The song grew clearer, the words almost intelligible, though still foreign. Lottie's eyes narrowed as she focused on the symbols around the arch, each one shifting slightly in response to the music.

"This is some kind of puzzle, isn't it?" she said, a realization dawning on her. "We need to match the melody with the symbols."

"Great," Penny said, rolling her eyes. "I can't read ancient musical notes."

Jasper stepped forward, his eyes lighting up as he studied the stone carvings. "Actually, I think I can help. These symbols are based on sound frequencies, like a musical scale. If I can match them to the melody..."

He paused, concentrating as the song began to play again. Slowly, he raised a hand to trace the symbols with his finger. "Here," he said, pointing to a symbol that matched a particular tone in the song. "This one represents the first note. And this one," he said, pointing to another, "matches the second."

The melody swelled, and the archway glowed brighter, its energy pulsing more strongly. Penny stepped back, watching with a mixture of awe and apprehension.

"This is insane," she muttered. "We're playing an ancient game of musical chairs with magic."

The Unlocking of the Arch

As Jasper matched more of the symbols to the melody, the air around them vibrated with energy. The soft voice that had been singing now shifted into a more cohesive tune, and the archway began to hum in harmony with it.

Suddenly, the arch's stone surface split with a loud crack, revealing a hidden passage beneath. The melody began to fade, and the soft voice stopped.

The archway had opened, and a shimmering light poured from the passage within, casting a gentle glow on their faces.

Lottie stepped forward cautiously, glancing back at the others. "I think we did it."

"Maybe," Penny said warily. "But that song... it felt like it was trying to pull us in."

Jasper nodded. "It was an enchantment. But we've solved it. We're through. Let's not waste time."

With a deep breath, the trio walked through the archway, entering the hidden passage. The fog outside seemed to pull back as they crossed the threshold, leaving behind the haunting melody.

The Other Side

The path on the other side of the arch was illuminated by soft, golden light that seemed to emanate from the stone walls themselves. The air here was different—clearer, fresher—but there was an unnatural stillness to it. No sounds of wildlife, no wind rustling the leaves, just an eerie quiet.

"I don't like how still it is," Penny muttered, glancing around warily. "It's like we're in some kind of ancient tomb."

"Careful, Penny," Lottie warned, her hand resting on the Bell of Guffaws. "We don't know what's ahead."

As they continued down the passage, the walls began to shift in color, from golden to deep violet, and the path began to widen, revealing a grand chamber. At the center of the chamber stood an ornate pedestal, on which rested an object that seemed to glow with otherworldly energy.

It was a crystal, large and radiant, with a swirling core of light inside. The chamber seemed to pulse with its energy, as if it was alive. The air around it hummed with a power they could feel deep in their bones.

“That’s it,” Jasper whispered. “The Heart of the Hollow.”

13

"The Heart of the Hollow"

The chamber was vast and silent, the golden light of the walls now replaced by a cool, violet glow. The crystal on the pedestal pulsed softly, as if breathing. Each beat sent ripples through the air, making the ground beneath them hum. It was both beautiful and unsettling. The trio stood motionless, entranced by the crystal's power.

"That's it," Jasper said, voice barely above a whisper. "The Heart of the Hollow... I can feel its magic. It's like nothing I've ever encountered."

Lottie stepped forward cautiously, her eyes fixed on the glowing crystal. "We've come this far. Whatever happens, we need to get it. It's the key to whatever's behind this whole forest mystery."

Penny, ever the skeptic, looked around nervously. "I don't know... this place feels wrong. Too still, too quiet.

Like something is waiting for us."

"Nothing ventured, nothing gained," Lottie replied, her voice steady. She reached out a hand toward the crystal. The air around it shimmered, and as her fingers brushed against its surface, a wave of warmth washed over her.

Suddenly, a voice—soft, but ancient—echoed through the chamber, reverberating in their minds.

"Do you dare awaken the Heart?"

The trio froze, the voice echoing louder now. The chamber seemed to grow darker as the crystal's glow intensified. "Who... who's speaking?" Penny whispered, her voice shaky.

"I am the Spirit of the Hollow," the voice continued. "I guard the Heart, the source of all magic in these woods. To take it is to claim the power of the forest itself, but not without consequence. Are you willing to face the price?"

Lottie, sensing the gravity of the situation, spoke up. "We're not here to take power. We need the Heart to understand what's happening in this forest. We're trying to stop something—something that's been hidden for a long time."

The voice paused, as if contemplating her words. "You seek answers. But the forest answers in its own way. Its truths are not always kind. Will you still proceed?"

Jasper exchanged a glance with the others. "We don't have much of a choice. If we want to stop whatever is wrong here, we need this."

"Very well," the Spirit intoned. "But know this: The Heart will show you the truth, and with it comes the burden of wisdom. What you learn here may be more than you are ready to bear."

The crystal pulsed once more, and a sudden gust of wind swept through the chamber. The ground trembled, and the trio braced themselves. The walls of the chamber cracked open, revealing swirling shadows within. The chamber's atmosphere shifted from serene to intense, and the very air felt thick with anticipation.

"Hold on to something!" Penny shouted, as a wave of energy surged from the Heart. The floor beneath them cracked open, and they were pulled into the darkness.

The Truth Revealed

They fell—plunged into an endless void of swirling light and shadow. It felt like time had stopped. The moment stretched into eternity. Then, with a sudden jolt, they landed softly on the ground. They were no longer in the chamber, but standing in a vast, open field—one that was eerily familiar, yet different.

The sky above them was a deep crimson, the ground beneath their feet covered in an unnatural mist. In the distance, a shadowy figure moved across the horizon, but it wasn't a person—more like a twisted silhouette that seemed to shift with every step it took.

"This is... wrong," Penny said, her voice barely a whisper. "This doesn't look like anything I've seen before."

Lottie's eyes darted around, searching for any clues. "This isn't just a vision... this is something deeper. The Heart isn't just showing us the forest—it's showing us the past."

Jasper, his face pale, stepped forward. "That figure... I know it. It's... it's the original guardian of the Hollow—the one who disappeared long ago."

The shadowy figure turned, its form becoming clearer. It was a tall, imposing figure cloaked in darkness, with eyes that burned like embers. It was familiar in a haunting way, like a forgotten memory clawing its way to the surface.

"You are the children of the ones who left," the figure said, its voice a deep, echoing whisper. "You have come to finish what was started. But you cannot undo what has already been done."

Lottie felt a chill run down her spine. "Who are you?"

The figure stepped closer, its form now fully visible. It was the shape of a long-lost ancestor—one of the original founders of the village, long believed to be lost to time. But this one... this one was corrupted, its once noble face now twisted by dark magic.

"I am the Guardian," it rasped. "But I was betrayed, and my soul was shattered. The Hollow's heart is what keeps me bound to this place—trapped between worlds. You must decide. Will you set me free... or will you destroy me?"

The mist around them swirled, and the ground beneath their feet began to pulse. The forest's magic—its very essence—was unraveling, and with it, the balance of the Hollow itself.

A Dreadful Decision

The trio exchanged uneasy looks, understanding the weight of the choice before them. The figure had once been a guardian, someone who had protected the forest, but now, it was something else—twisted and consumed by the magic that bound it.

"Is setting you free what we're meant to do?" Lottie asked, her voice trembling with the realization of what it might mean.

"Yes," the Guardian's voice was low, but pleading. "But it may cost you. The magic of the Hollow will change. It will never be the same again. I was once the protector, but in my fall, I became the curse. If you destroy me, the Hollow will remain in eternal torment."

Penny frowned. "We can't destroy you. But can we really trust you after everything?"

Jasper stepped forward, his hand on his chin. "There's no easy answer here. But what we've learned is that we can't keep running from the truth. We have to make a choice—whether to risk setting things right or letting this curse continue."

14

"The Choice of the Hollow"

The silence was suffocating as the trio stood before the twisted Guardian, its dark form looming like a specter of forgotten sorrow. The air felt thick with the weight of the decision that hung over them like an unshakable storm cloud.

Lottie, Penny, and Jasper exchanged glances, each feeling the crushing weight of the choice that lay before them. Set the Guardian free, and risk undoing the balance of the forest—and possibly the world itself—or destroy it, leaving the Hollow in eternal torment. The consequences of either choice seemed impossible to predict.

"I don't trust it," Penny muttered, her voice tight with suspicion. "This creature... this Guardian—who knows what will happen if we set it free?"

Jasper took a step closer to the Guardian, his eyes focused on its hollow, burning gaze. "It's not about trust, Penny. It's about what the forest needs. The magic of the Hollow was never meant to be corrupted. If we destroy the Guardian, we may just be locking the curse in place forever."

Lottie folded her arms, her mind racing. She knew that something wasn't right about the whole situation. The Hollow had always been a place of enchantment and mystery, but now it was as though the very soul of the forest was caught in a battle between light and dark. Could they really trust the Guardian? And if not, what was the right path?

"You're right, Jasper," Lottie said, her voice firm, though her uncertainty remained. "But there's something off about all of this. If this Guardian was once a protector, what happened to it? Why is it now a twisted shadow?"

The Guardian's voice rumbled through the air, low and sorrowful. "I was deceived, as you are deceived now. The forest was once my charge, my sacred duty. But those who came before you—those who betrayed me—have corrupted the heart. I have been bound by their treachery."

The figure shifted, its cloak of shadows swirling around it like a living thing. "The Hollow is dying because of their mistake. It is only through my release that balance can be restored. But the price of freedom... it is greater than you can imagine."

Lottie's brow furrowed. "What price? What do you mean?"

The Guardian's eyes flickered with a mix of sorrow and regret. "The magic that binds me to this place is tied to the life force of the Hollow. If I am set free, I will become the guardian once more, but the forest will lose its magic. The very essence of the Hollow—the enchantment, the life that flows through it—will fade. It will become a shadow of what it once was."

Penny's eyes widened in horror. "You're saying that if we set you free, the forest will die?"

"No," the Guardian replied, its voice now tinged with something softer. "Not die. But it will change. The magic will no longer pulse with life. The Hollow will become... mortal. It will be like any other place in the world."

Jasper took a deep breath, his mind racing. "So, if we destroy you, the forest lives—but in torment. If we set you free, the forest will lose its magic forever. Neither option is perfect."

Lottie's heart sank. The world felt smaller in that moment, as if the forest itself was holding its breath, waiting for them to decide.

The Revelation of the Heart

Before Lottie could respond, the crystal at the center of the Hollow flared to life, its glow intensifying until it seemed to flood the entire landscape. The light bathed the Guardian in a soft, ethereal glow, illuminating the haunting sadness in its eyes.

"I have carried this curse for too long," the Guardian said, its voice now full of sorrow. "And it is not only my burden—it is the burden of all who live within this Hollow. But the time has come. The magic that holds me here is weakening. The forest is dying, and so am I. If you do not act now, the Hollow will fall into a deep slumber, and all that remains will be memories of what once was."

The air shimmered, and for a brief moment, Lottie, Penny, and Jasper saw visions of the Hollow as it had been—lush, vibrant, full of life and light. The trees danced in the wind, the river sparkled under the sun, and creatures of all shapes and sizes frolicked beneath the canopy.

But then, the vision shifted. The trees grew twisted, their bark darkened, and the river became a sluggish, murky stream. The creatures disappeared, replaced by shadows and decay. The Hollow—once a place of magic—was dying.

“If I remain bound, it will be too late,” the Guardian whispered. “But if you set me free... you will be left with a decision you cannot undo. The forest will fade into the past.”

Lottie, her heart heavy with the weight of the decision, stepped forward. “We can’t let it die,” she said, her voice filled with determination. “But we can’t destroy the Guardian either. There must be another way.”

A New Path

Suddenly, a soft breeze rustled through the trees, and the faintest glimmer of light appeared above the crystal. It shimmered, flickering like the last remnants of a dying star, then expanded into a swirling vortex of energy.

A new voice—gentler, wiser—spoke.

“There is another way, child.”

The trio turned, startled by the voice, but it came from the very heart of the Hollow, from the crystal itself. Slowly, it began to form a shape—a figure emerging from the light. It was a woman, her form glowing with the same ethereal light as the crystal, her eyes soft and knowing.

“I am the Spirit of the Hollow,” she said, her voice both soothing and powerful. “I have watched over this land for eons. The Guardian’s curse is not his alone, but the result of an ancient mistake. The balance you seek does not lie in freeing him or destroying him—it lies in mending the forest, in restoring the Hollow to its true nature.”

Lottie’s breath caught in her throat. “What do you mean?”

The Spirit smiled, a warm, calming presence. "There is a third option. A path that only those who carry the wisdom of the Hollow can walk. You must merge the Heart's magic with the land once more—restore its pulse, its essence, and the Guardian's power will be rebalanced. You will be the new guardians of the Hollow, the ones who guide it into a new era."

15

"The Restoration of the Hollow"

The air seemed to shimmer with the weight of the Spirit's words. The idea of merging the Heart's magic with the land—of becoming guardians themselves—felt like both a monumental responsibility and a glimmer of hope in a seemingly impossible situation. The trio stood before the Spirit of the Hollow, trying to process the gravity of what she had proposed.

"You... you want us to merge with the Heart?" Penny's voice was tinged with disbelief. "But how? We're not... magical. We're just us."

The Spirit's smile softened. "You may not be as you believe. The Hollow has chosen you. It has called you, and you have answered. You are the ones who will shape the future of this place. The Heart has always been a living force, and it is through the hearts of those who truly understand its power that it can be restored."

Jasper stepped forward, his eyes wide with wonder. "But how does this work? How do we restore the balance?"

The Spirit gestured toward the crystal, its glow intensifying with every word. "You will place your hands upon the Heart, and the magic of the Hollow will merge with your own. Through your bond, the land will heal. The Guardian's power will be rebalanced, and the forest will be restored. But this will not be easy. It will require great strength and an unwavering bond between you."

Lottie's heart raced. This was their moment—the chance to restore the Hollow to its former glory. But the weight of it all pressed heavily upon her. Could they truly do this? Could they save the Hollow and the Guardian, without losing themselves in the process?

"I know we can do this," she said, her voice steady with resolve. "We've come this far together. And we won't give up now."

Penny nodded, her usual sarcasm replaced by a rare sincerity. "I might not be a fan of all this 'magical destiny' stuff, but if it means fixing this place and stopping whatever curse is on it, I'm in."

Jasper adjusted his glasses and gave a determined smile. "I've never backed down from a challenge. Let's do this."

The Ritual of Restoration

The trio approached the Heart of the Hollow, its glow now brighter than ever, pulsing with an almost sentient rhythm. The Guardian, once a twisted shadow of its former self, now stood in silence, its dark form still, as if awaiting their decision.

With one final glance at each other, they each reached out and placed their hands on the Heart. The moment their palms made contact with the smooth surface of the crystal, a rush of energy surged through them. It was as though the very essence of the Hollow was flowing into their veins—wild, untamed, but also grounding, connecting them to the land in ways they could never have imagined.

The magic of the forest surged with such intensity that it felt like the air itself had become alive. The ground trembled beneath their feet as visions of the Hollow's past, present, and future flashed before their eyes. They saw the lush forests, the vibrant wildlife, and the villages that had once thrived within the Hollow. But they also saw the darkness that had crept in—the betrayal that had shattered the balance, the Guardian's fall into corruption, and the slow decay of the forest as it suffered the consequences of that broken trust.

The forest's heartbeat—the very pulse of the Hollow—was weak, faltering. But as they stood there, hands on the Heart, they felt it begin to strengthen. The energy that had once been chaotic and wild began to settle, becoming more focused, more grounded. They were channeling the magic, not as individuals, but as one unified force. They could feel their bond to the forest—and to each other—grow stronger with every passing moment.

Suddenly, the Guardian's voice echoed through their minds, but it was no longer filled with sorrow or darkness. It was clear and calm, full of gratitude.

"You have done it," the Guardian said, its tone now gentle and full of relief. "The Hollow's magic is restored. The curse is broken. You have freed me from the chains of my past. And with your help, the forest will live again."

The ground beneath them seemed to hum with life, the pulse of the Hollow growing stronger, the air clearer, and the mist lifting from the trees. The dark, twisted branches that had once plagued the forest now began to heal, turning vibrant and green once more. The river, once sluggish and murky, sparkled in the sunlight. The creatures of the forest reappeared, their forms materializing from the mist, moving with an energy and vitality that had been lost for so long.

The Awakening

As the trio stood in awe, the Spirit of the Hollow stepped forward, her glowing form radiant with the energy of the restored forest. “The Hollow is whole once more,” she said, her voice like the rustling of leaves in the wind. “And so, you have become the new guardians of this land. The magic that flows through you now is part of the forest’s essence. You will protect it, nurture it, and ensure that it remains balanced for generations to come.”

Lottie, Penny, and Jasper exchanged stunned looks. They had done it. They had restored the Hollow. But more than that, they had become a part of it. They were now bound to the forest, its guardians and protectors, connected to the very heart of the land.

But as the weight of their new roles settled in, a sense of peace washed over them. They were no longer just outsiders wandering through the forest. They were its protectors. They would carry its legacy, its magic, and its secrets forward.

As the Spirit of the Hollow began to fade, her voice lingered in the air. "Remember, the forest is not just a place. It is a living entity, and it will always be with you. Guide it with wisdom and love, and it will continue to thrive."

And with that, the Spirit vanished, leaving only the whisper of the wind in her wake.

A New Dawn

The sun began to rise, casting its golden light over the restored forest. The Hollow was alive again—its magic restored, its balance regained. The trio stood at the edge of the clearing, the Heart of the Hollow now pulsing quietly in the center, its glow steady and serene.

"We did it," Penny said, a smile tugging at the corners of her lips. "We actually did it."

Lottie's eyes sparkled with both pride and exhaustion. "We sure did. But now, we've got a new job. One that's a little more permanent."

Jasper adjusted his glasses with a grin. "Guess we're officially the new guardians of the Hollow, huh? That's a job I'm definitely not going to put on my resume."

Lottie laughed, her heart lighter than it had been in ages. "I think this is one job we can all be proud of."

Together, they turned toward the heart of the Hollow, ready to face whatever challenges the future might hold. The forest was alive once more, and they—its new guardians—were ready to protect it for as long as it would need them.

16

CHAPTER CRAFTERS

Sharvaeshvar - MAIN AUTHOR

Tharunaswanth - Author

Sarvesh - Author

Hemachander - Author

www.ingramcontent.com/pod-product-compliance
Lightning Source LLC
LaVergne TN
LVHW041115150826
845673LV00007B/2055

* 9 7 9 8 8 9 7 2 4 4 9 9 7 *